I look in the mirror.

Skinny.

Ugly.

I want to look like David Beckham.
I want to look like Cristiano Ronaldo

At least I can't see how short I am.

I wanted to play well today.
I read this stuff online.

Go for it!
Hold your head up!

Right!

I went for it…

…and I missed an open goal.

I held my head up…

…and fell over.

Mum taps on my door.
She says, "I got the stuff you wanted."
I look at the body spray and DVD.
I think about the TV ads.

I think, "You're a skinny,
ugly freak, Steve Jones."

I look in the mirror.

Fat.

Ugly.

I want to look like Cheryl Cole.
I want to look like Katy Perry.

At least ginger hair doesn't
show in the dark.

I wanted to look good tonight.
I hardly ate anything all week.

I spent pounds on fake tan and make-up.

Right!

No chocolate all week…
      …but my new jeans were still too tight.

A new tan and make-up…
                …but I still looked ugly.

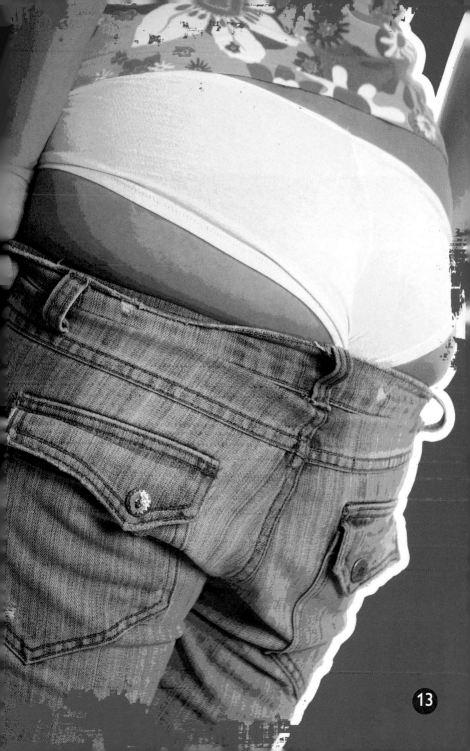

13

I sat in the corner all night.

No one talked to me.

I want to be thin and pretty.
Then everybody would talk to me.

I say, "You're a fat, ugly freak,
Lizzie Owen."

It's Monday. We've got art.
I'm working on my project.

Miss Allen says, "This looks amazing, Steve."
She says, "You should enter the design
competition."

I look at the screen.
I go bright red.
I say, "It's OK, Miss. I'll leave it."

That night I watch my football DVD.
I look in the mirror.

Skinny.

Short.

Rubbish at sport.

I'm no good.

It's Monday. I'm looking at the notice board.

Mr. King says, "You should try out for the show, Lizzie."
He says, "You're a good singer."

I go bright red.
I say, "It's OK, Sir. I'll leave it."

That night I look in the mirror.

Fat.

Ugly.

Ginger hair.

I wish I was thin with dark hair.
Then I could try out for the show.

It's Friday lunchtime.
I go to the art room.

Lizzie Owen is working
on her project.
She doesn't see me come in.

I like Lizzie Owen.
She's funny and kind.

Lizzie is singing to herself.
She's a great singer.

I say, "Hi, Lizzie."

She stops singing and
goes bright red.

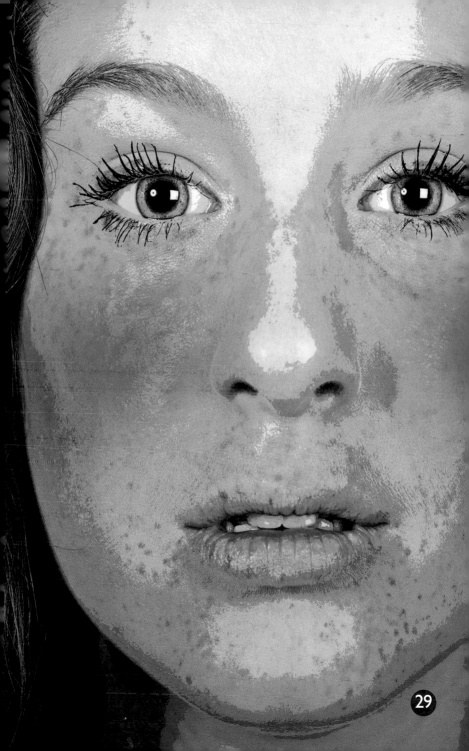

Oh no!
Steve Jones just heard me singing.
I was working on my project and
I didn't see him come in.
He said hi and then he went bright red.

I like Steve.
He has cool ideas.
I must look at his project.
I bet it's amazing!

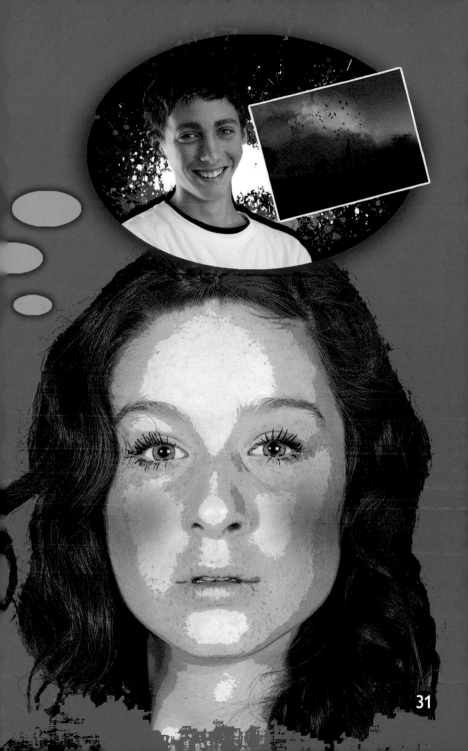

Lizzie comes over.
She looks at my project.

Lizzie says, "Wow. That looks great.
My dad's a designer. He would give
you a job like that."

Then Lizzie looks sad.

She says, "I wish I looked like those girls."

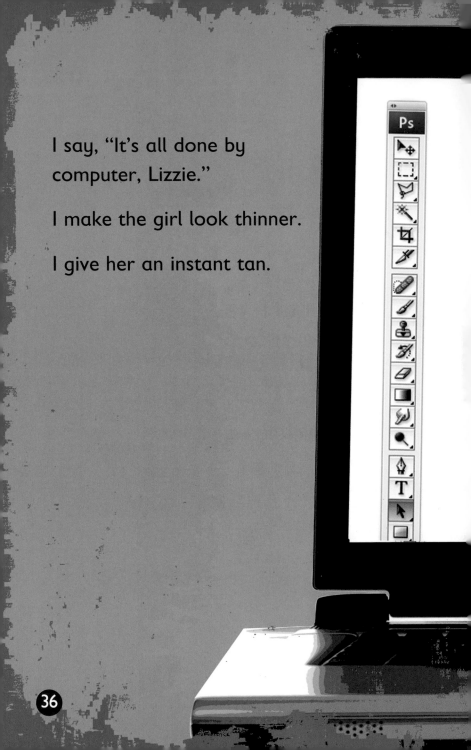

I say, "It's all done by computer, Lizzie."

I make the girl look thinner.

I give her an instant tan.

I look at Steve's screen.
He says, "You're a really good singer.
You should try out for the show."

I say, "I don't look right."

Steve holds up his phone.
I laugh.
I say, "Don't, Steve!"

A minute later I'm on the computer screen.

I look at the screen.

I say, "Wow. What did you do, Steve?"

He says, "Nothing Lizzie. It's all you."

I sit next to Steve.
I feel so happy.
I say, "You have cool ideas.
You should enter that design competition."

Lizzie gives me a big smile.
I smile back at her.
I say, "Maybe I will!"

MIRROR - WHAT'S NEXT?

Steve won't enter a design competition because he doesn't play football well.

Lizzie won't try out as a singer in the show because she has ginger hair.

Think of something you are good at.
What could you do with this skill?
Why aren't you doing it?
Does your reason make sense?

Set yourself a goal – and go for it!

Lizzie and Steve describe themselves as skinny, short, fat and ginger. They describe each other as funny, kind and cool.

Fat
Short
Glasses
Freckles
Pale

Funny
Cute
Loyal
Cool
Smiley

• Look in a mirror. Write down five words to describe what you see.

• Ask your partner to write down five words they would use to describe you.

44

• Compare the two lists. Do friends make good mirrors?

WALLFLOWERS
IN A GROUP

"Wallflowers" cling to the
wall at parties! Look at pages
14 and 15. Role-play the scene
at the party.
Give the guests names and think about
their characters. What do the guests
think about Lizzie?

• She's shy/boring.
• She thinks she's too good for us.
• She looks miserable.
• I didn't notice her!

What does Lizzie think?

AD LAND
ON YOUR OWN / WITH A PARTNER / IN A GROUP

Look at pages 8 to 9. The advert is saying:
If you use this spray, girls will want to be with
you. The DVD cover is
saying:
If you watch this DVD, you
will play like David
Beckham.

Find an advert and answer
these questions.

• What is it selling?
• What is it saying?
• How realistic is this message?
   (Will the spray attract girls? Will watching
   a DVD make you a great football player?)

IF YOU ENJOYED
THIS BOOK,
TRY THESE OTHER
RIGHT NOW!
BOOKS.

Alisha's online messages to new girl Sam get nastier and nastier. Will anyone help Sam?

Mark's fighter jet is under attack. There's only one way to escape...

Lucy and Lloyd were in love, but now it's over. So why is Lloyd always watching her?

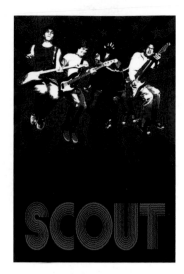

It's Saturday night.
Two angry guys. Two knives.
There's going to be a fight.

Tonight is the band's big
chance. Tonight, a record
company scout is at their gig!

Ed's platoon is under attack.
Another soldier is in danger.
Ed must risk his own life to
save him.

It's just an old, empty house.
Lauren must spend the night
inside. Just Lauren and the
ghost...

47

JOYRIDE

Dan sees the red car.
The keys are inside. Dan says
to Andy, Sam and Jess,
"Want to go for a drive?"

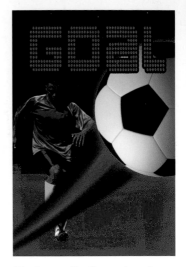

Today is Carl's trial with
City. There's just one place
up for grabs. But today,
everything is going wrong!

FRIEND

Sophie hates this new town.
She misses her friends.
There's nowhere to skate!

DUMPED

Tonight, Vicky must make a
choice. Stay in London with
her boyfriend Chris. Or start
a new life in Australia.